CW01507151

Spring Comes Riding in a Carriage

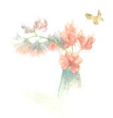

Riichi Yokomitsu + Atsuko Ito

"Spring Comes Riding in a Carriage"
first appeared in the magazine *Josei* in August of 1926

RIICHI YOKOMITSU

Born in Fukushima Prefecture in 1898, Yokomitsu was sometimes referred to as "The God of Literature" even during his lifetime. He was expelled from the Department of Political Science and Economics at Waseda University and became a disciple of Kan Kikuchi, making his literary debut in 1923 with "A Fly" and "The Sun," which were published at the same time. His representative works include "Machine" and "Melancholy Journey."

Illustrations: ATSUKI ITO

Ito became an illustrator after graduating from the Faculty of Education at Bunkyo University and working as a nursery school teacher. Having completed the hands-on book design course at Gallery DAZZLE, Ito published *Love Letters in 26 Characters*.

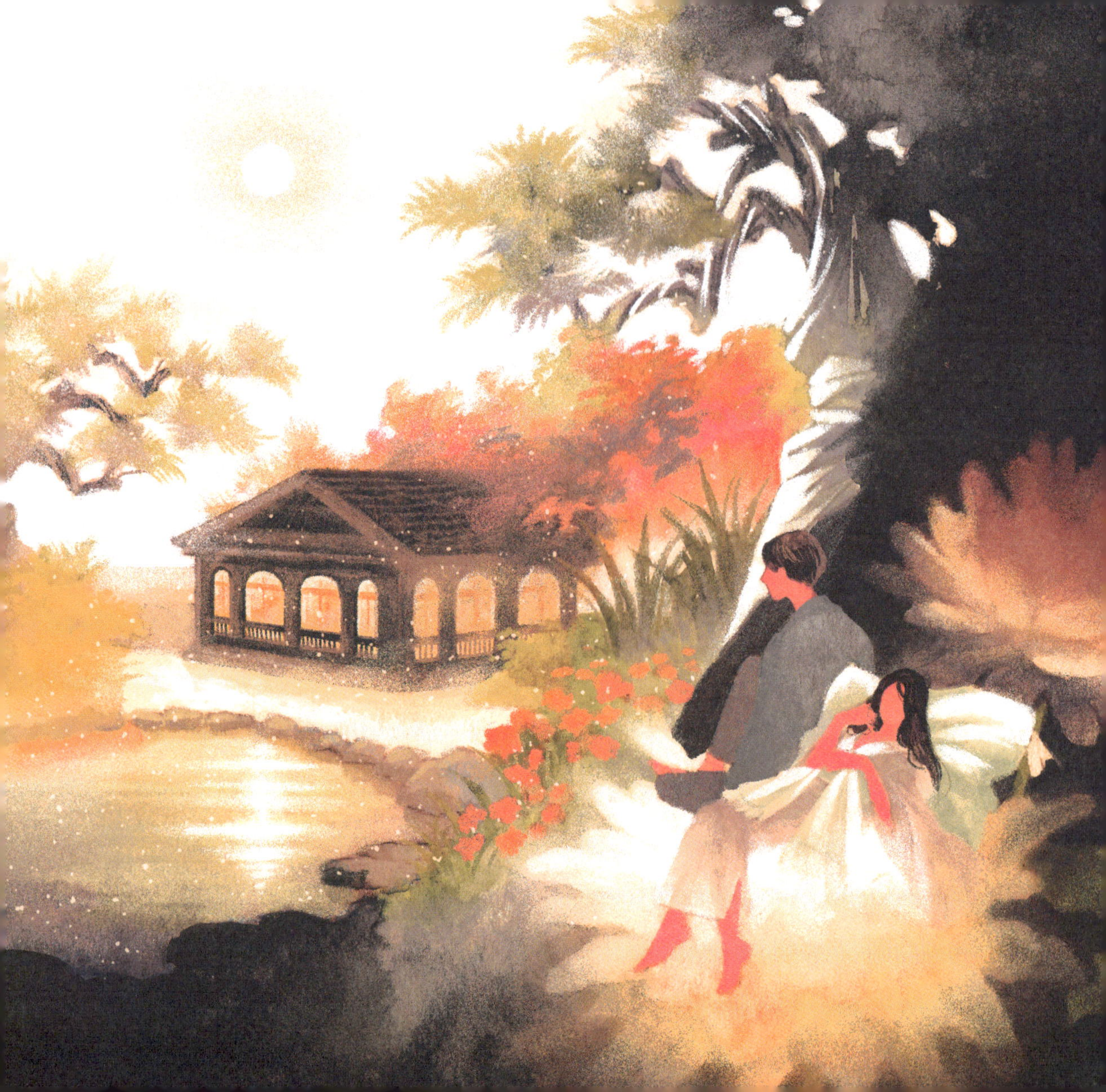

The pine trees on the coast began to rustle in the bitter wind of late autumn. In one corner of the garden, a cluster of small dahlias withered away.

He stood beside the bed where his wife lay, gazing at the sluggish turtle in the pond. When it swam about, the bright light reflected in the surface of the water rippled over the dry rocks.

"Look, dear, how beautifully the pine needles glimmer in the light," she said.

"So you were looking at the trees."

"Yes."

"I was looking at the turtle."

They very nearly lapsed back into silence.

"You've been lying there all this time, and that's all you have to say? That the pine needles look pretty in the light?"

"Yes. After all, I've made up my mind not to think about anything anymore."

"Surely no one can lie in bed without thinking about something."

"Well, I can't help having thoughts, of course. I'm itching to get better so I can do some laundry at the well, give it a good scrub."

"Laundry?" He burst out laughing at his wife's peculiar desire. "You're a funny one. After everything you've put me through, you want to do laundry, of all things?"

"I just miss being that strong and healthy. You're an unfortunate man, aren't you?"

He murmured his assent.

First he thought back on the four or five years he had struggled with her family before they finally gave in and let him marry her. Then he thought about the two painful years he had spent trapped between his mother and his wife, and how, just when his mother had died and they were left to live by themselves, his wife had become suddenly bedridden with a respiratory malady. And he recalled this past year of wretched travails which had followed.

"I see what you mean. Now I feel like doing some laundry myself."

"You know, I wouldn't mind if I died right now. But I want to do more to repay your kindness before I go. It's been weighing on me so much these days."

"And just what do you suppose you'd do for me?"

"Well, I'd look after you, for a start..."

"And?"

"And there are so many more things I'd do."

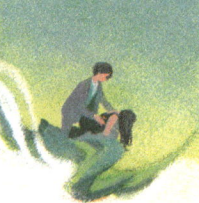

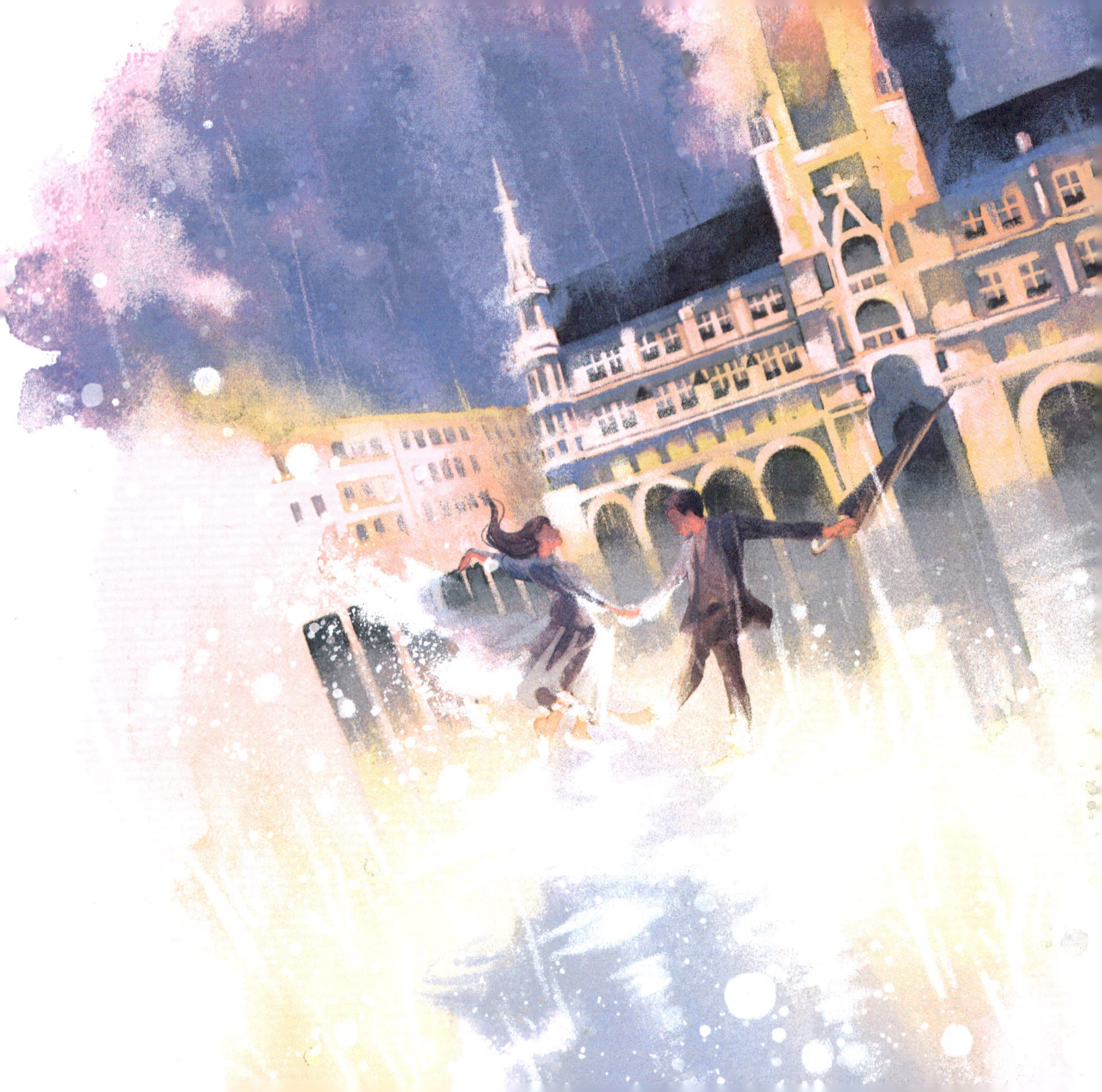

But she's not going to get better, he thought.

"I don't care about anything like that. If you ask me, all I want—yes, all I want is to take a trip to Germany. Somewhere around Munich. And it has to be rainy, otherwise I'm not interested."

"I want to go with you." Even as she said this, a cough undulated through her body.

"You need to rest."

"No, no, I want to walk. Come on, please, help me up."

"You mustn't."

"I don't care if I die."

"There's no use in dying."

"It's fine, I don't mind."

"Just stay still. And think of a word, just one adjective, for how beautiful those pine needles are when they shine in the light—that'll be your life's work."

His wife with-
drew into silence. He
stood up, trying to think of
a gentler subject that would raise
her spirits.

The afternoon waves were crashing
against distant rocks, sending up spray. Listing
to one side, a lone boat disappeared around the tip of
the sharp promontory. At the water's edge, two children sat
like crumpled scraps of paper amid the rich indigo of the break-
ers, steaming hot sweet potatoes in their hands.

He had never before wished to escape from the waves of hardship
that came rolling over him one after another—for he felt that these
waves of torment, each with its own unique quality, sprung from the
primal part of his own bodily existence. He was determined to scruti-
nize the pain, to hone his senses and savor each sensation like someone rolling a lump of sugar over their tongue. And at the end, he would
ask: which had been the sweetest?

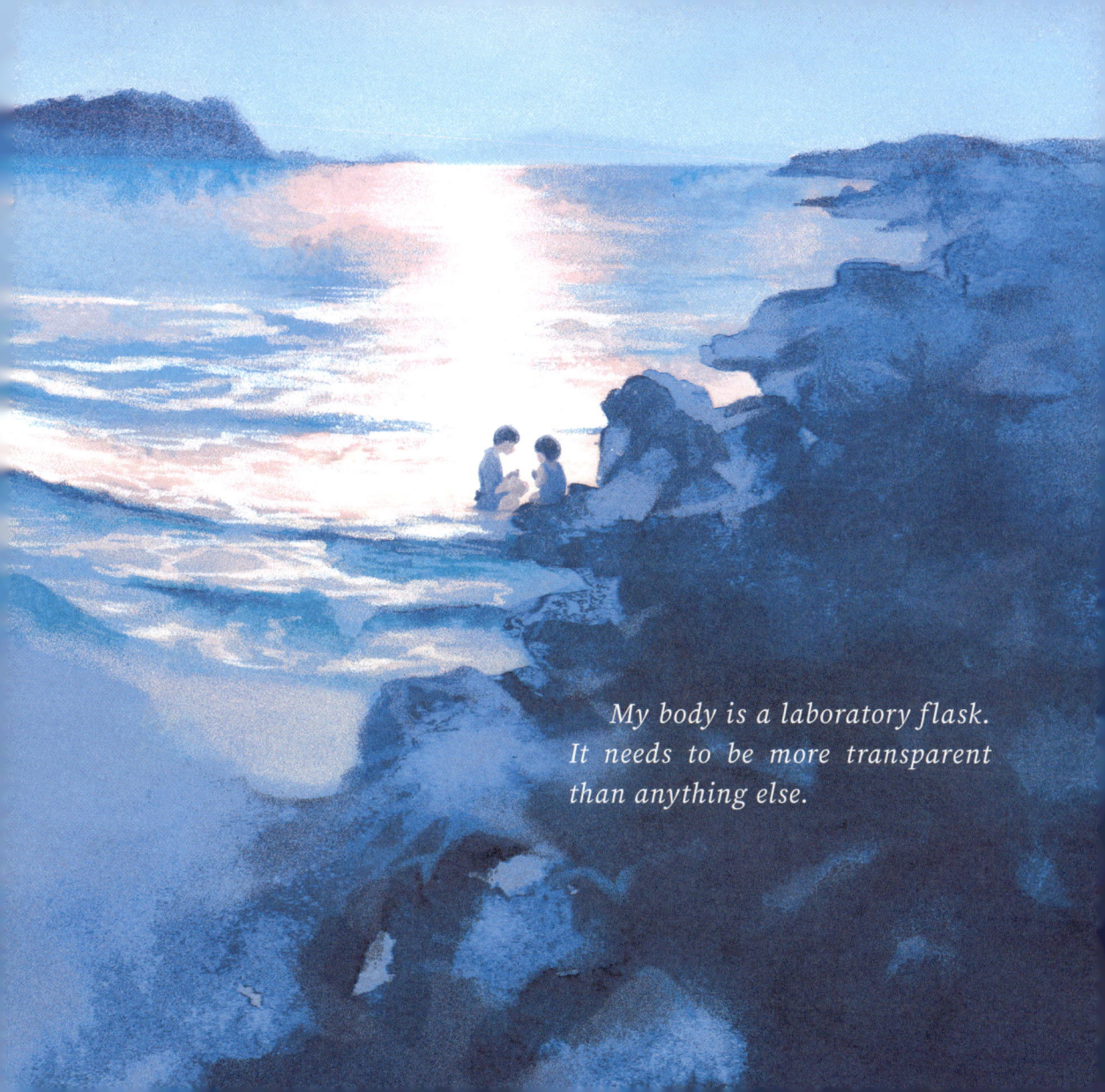

My body is a laboratory flask.
It needs to be more transparent
than anything else.

The dahlia stems were languishing on the ground like a tangle of shriveled rope. Gusts of salty wind blew over the horizon all day long, bringing winter with them.

Twice each day he went out in search of the fresh giblets his wife craved, walking through the clouds of sand and dust swept up by the wind. He called on every poulterer in the seaside town, peering over their yellow chopping blocks and surveying the yards beyond, before asking, "Giblets. Got any giblets?"

When he was lucky, the poulterer would bring out offal like gems of agate from the ice, and he would stride gallantly home to line up the spoils beside his wife's pillow.

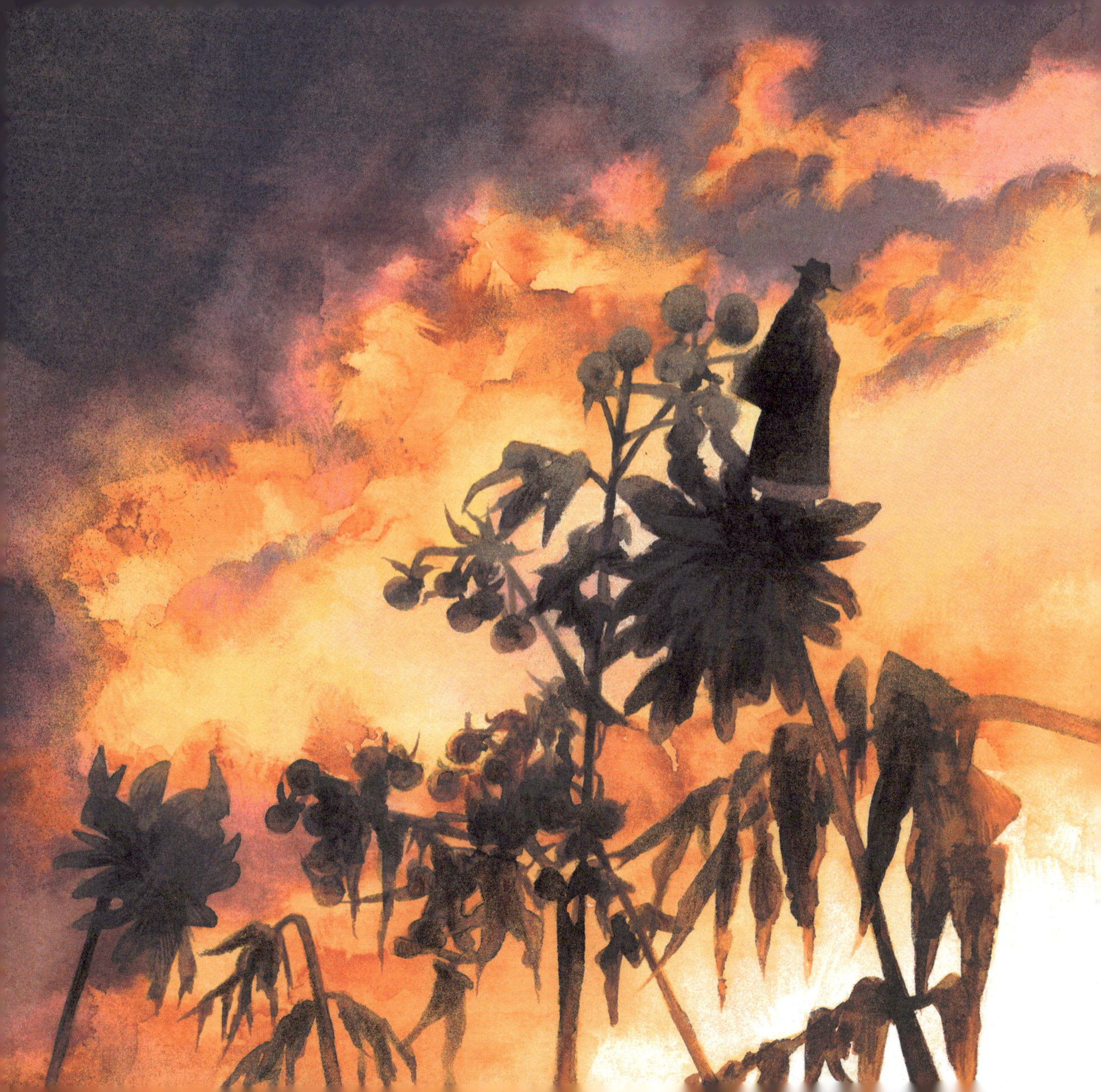

"This one shaped like a teardrop is a pigeon's kidney. This glossy piece of liver was plucked right out of a living duck. This one looks just like a lip that's been bitten off, and see this tiny greenish egg? It's like a piece of jade from Mount Kunlun."

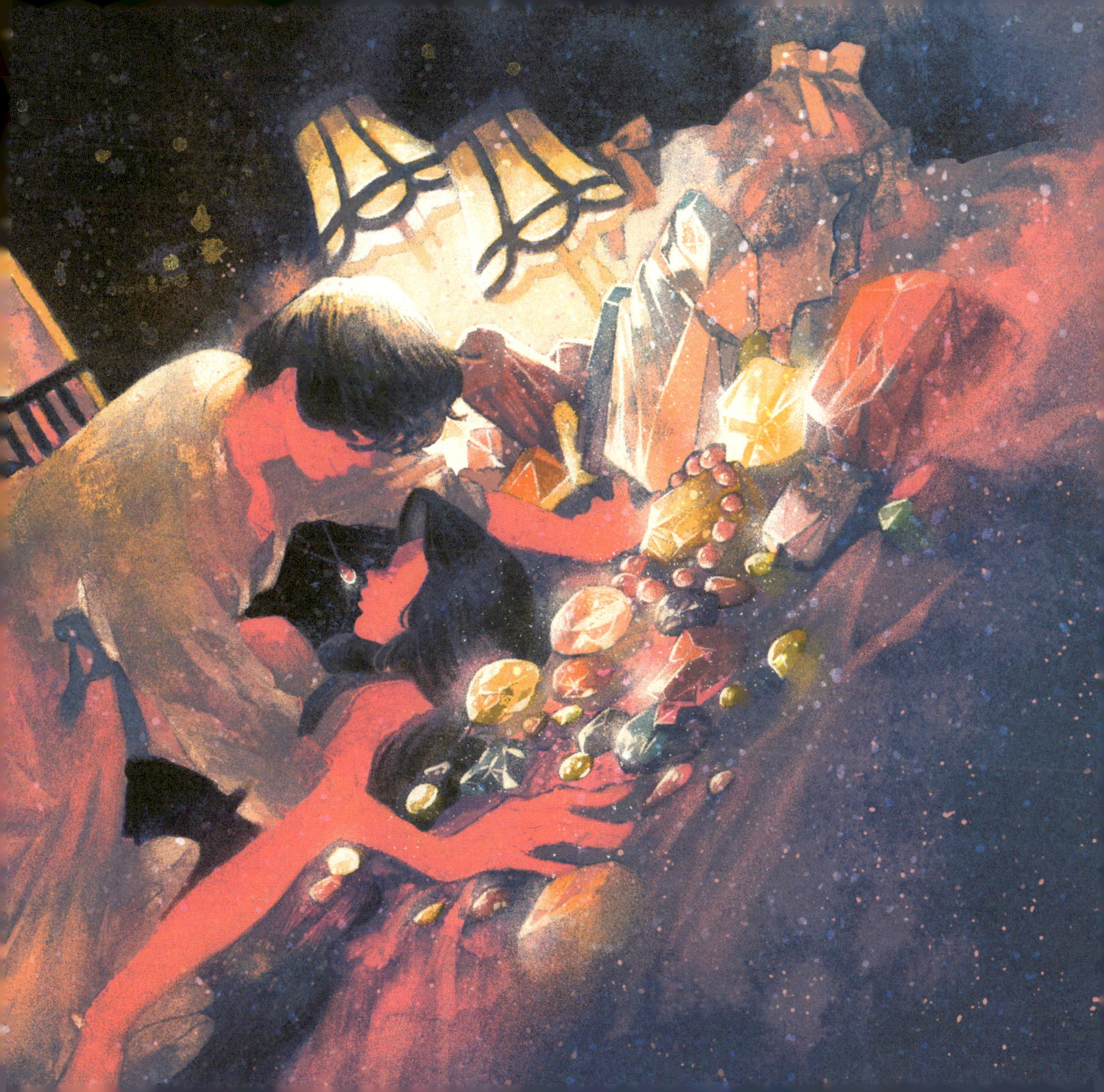

Then, roused by his eloquence, his wife would squirm feverishly in anticipation of the feast, as if she were urging him on to kiss her for the first time. At this point he would ruthlessly snatch away the giblets and toss them straight into a pot.

From where she lay behind the lattice of the bed, which surrounded her like a cage, his wife watched the steam rise from the boiling pot with a faint smile on her face.

"When I look at you from over here, you're a rather strange beast," he said.

"A beast! In spite of all this, I'm still your wife, you know."

"Hm. A wife in a cage, hungry for organ meat. There's always a whiff of brutality about you, somehow, no matter the situation."

"Look who's talking. You're a rational man, sometimes brutally so— all you ever think about is how you wish you could leave my side."

"That's just the suspicious theorizing of someone in a cage."

To elude his wife's keen perception, which never missed even the faintest flicker of a wrinkle smoldering on his brow, of late he inevitably found himself falling back on this conclusion. Still, sometimes her argument veered precipitously toward his weak point, penetrating his defenses and prowling around inside him.

Not that he always let it go without a rejoinder:

"Honestly, it's true, I don't like sitting by your side. Consumption isn't exactly a joyous thing, after all. Think about it. Even when I do leave your bedside, I just go around and around this garden in circles. I'm always tied to your bed, and I have no choice but to roam around within the circumference of that leash. It's pitiful, that's what it is—what else could you call a situation like that?"

"You just… You just want to go out and have fun, don't you?" she said bitterly.

"Don't you want to have fun?"

"I know you want to fool around with other women."

"Even if that were true, so what?"

When they reached that point in the conversation, his wife typically broke down in tears. It brought him back to himself, and he was forced to change tack and try ever so gently to dismantle her argument.

"I admit it, I don't like having to be by your bedside all day long. That's why I'm going around and around this same old garden trying to make you better as soon as humanly possible, isn't it? This isn't easy for me, you know."

"But you're only doing it for yourself. It's not because you care about me, not one bit."

Whenever his wife pressed him like this, he was, naturally, crushed by her argument. But was he really gritting his teeth and enduring this agony solely for his own sake?

"Fair enough. You're right, I must be putting up with all this for my own sake. But look, who put me in this position in the first place? If it weren't for you, I would never play at being a zookeeper like this. So who exactly am I doing that for? You think I stay here for anyone but you? Please."

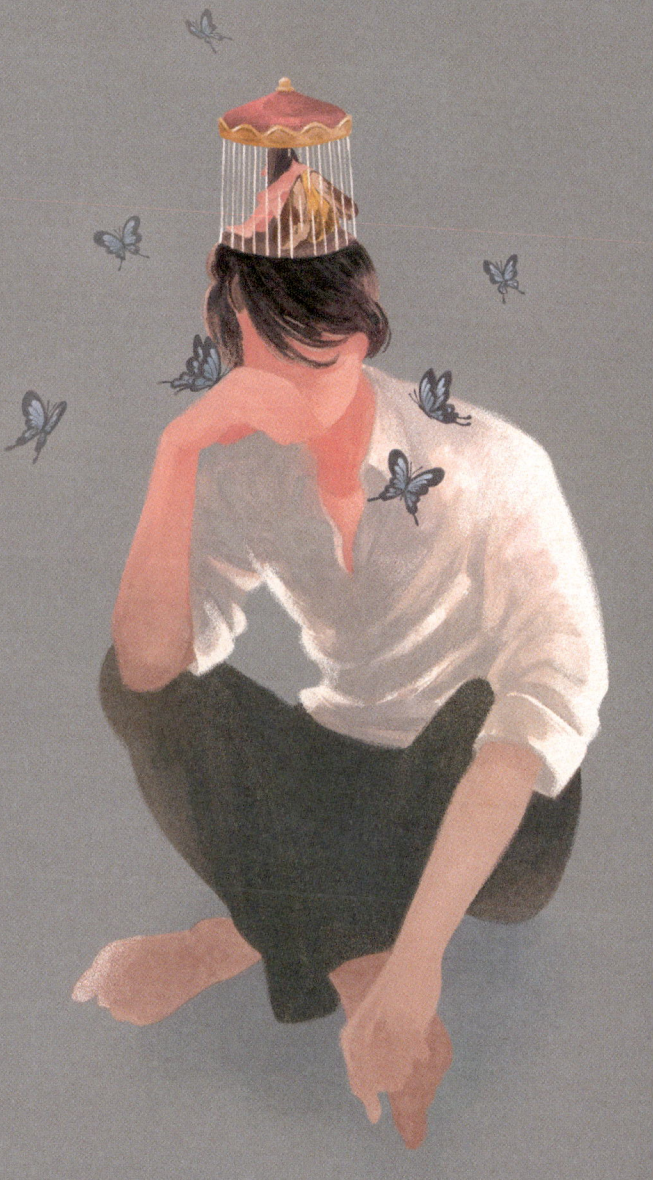

On nights like this, his wife's fever invariably shot up to around 102. Having made his position plain, he would now have to sit by her bedside all night long, filling and refilling her ice bag. And yet nearly every day he found himself forced to continue trotting out these confounded explanations in order to make her understand why he might need a break.

He went to another room to work, since he had to earn enough to eat and to care for the invalid. Whenever he did so, however, she assailed him again with the suspicion of the caged.

"Why are you so eager to be away from me? You've only come in here three times today. And I know why. That's exactly the kind of man you are."

"Come now, what do you expect me to do? I have to buy medicine and food to make you better. No one's going to pay me for sitting around all day. You want me to do some kind of magic trick, is that it?"

"But you can do your work in here, can't you?" she insisted.

"No, I really can't. The only way I can get any work done is when I've stopped thinking about you, even for the briefest moment."

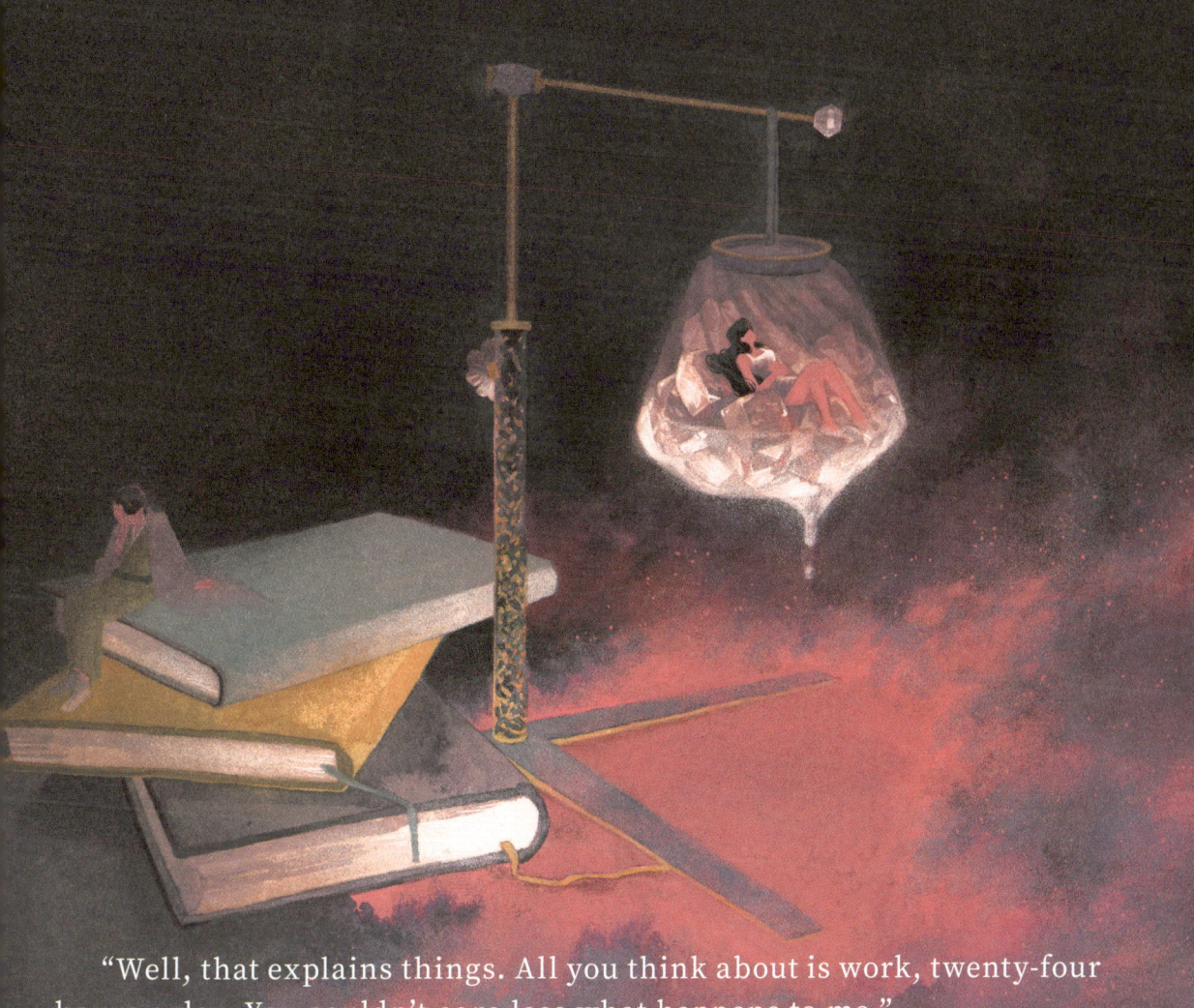

"Well, that explains things. All you think about is work, twenty-four hours a day. You couldn't care less what happens to me."

"It's my work that's your enemy, not me. But the fact is, your enemy is constantly laboring to keep you alive."

"I'm lonely."

"Everyone's lonely sometimes."

"It's all very well for you. You have your work. I don't have anything."

"Why not look for something, then?"

"I can't find anything but you. All I do is lie here, staring up at the ceiling."

"Give it a rest, please. Let's just agree that we're both lonely. I have a deadline. If I don't finish today, who knows how much trouble I'll cause them."

"There, you've shown your true colors. Deadlines are more important to you than I am."

"No, see, a deadline is like a notice on the wall that obliterates any and all extenuating circumstances. Now that I've seen the bill and taken on the job, I have to ignore my own circumstances, no matter what."

"There you are, as rational as ever. You're always like that. I hate people who intellectualize everything."

"As long as you live in my house, you're just as responsible for these notices on the wall as I am."

"Can't you simply turn them down?"

"But then how would I make a living? How would we survive?"

"I'd rather die than feel you grow so cold and indifferent."

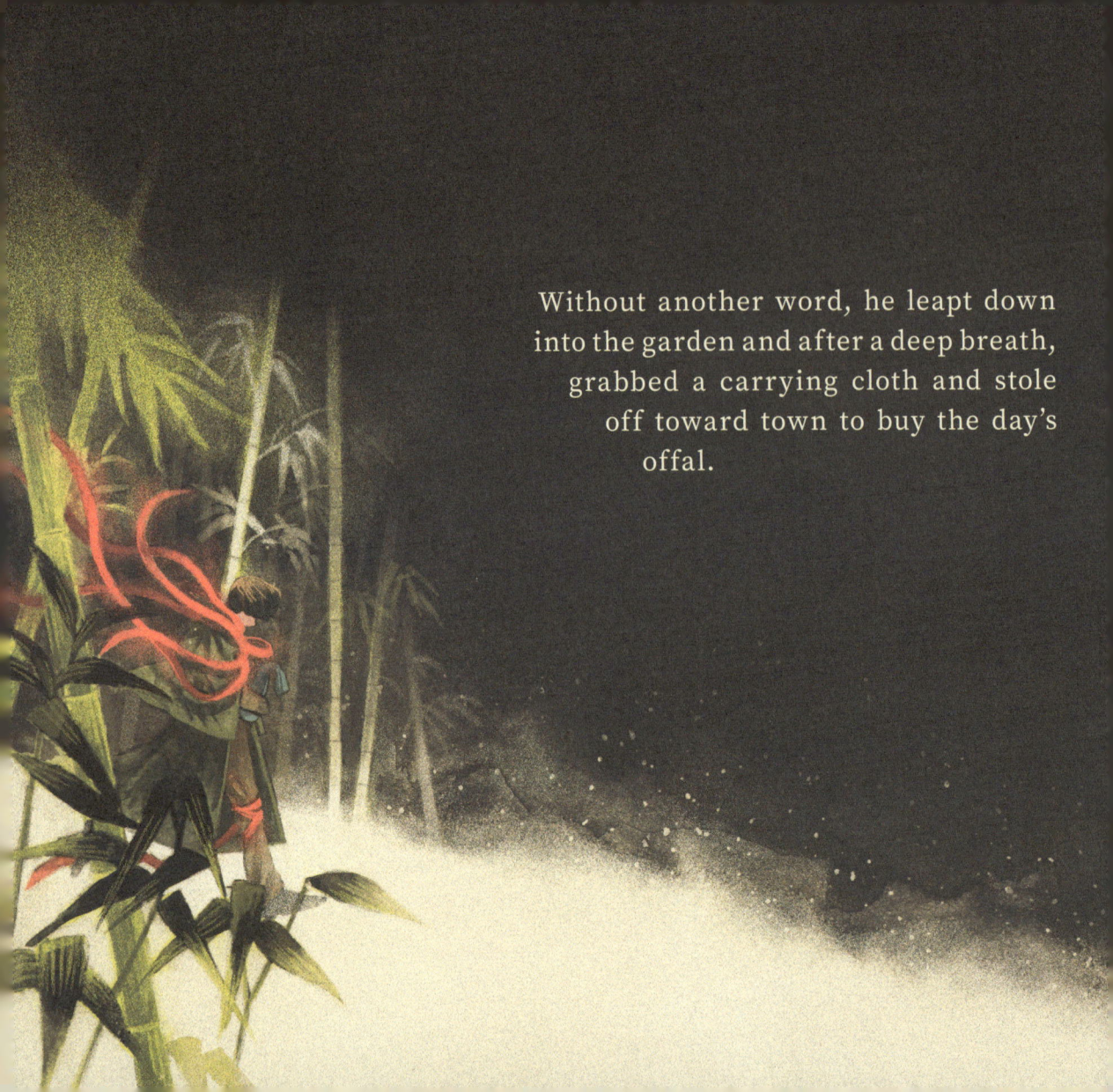

Without another word, he leapt down into the garden and after a deep breath, grabbed a carrying cloth and stole off toward town to buy the day's offal.

But the argument of the caged constantly, relentlessly pursued his own rationale—the argument of the one who is tied to the cage, circling around it endlessly—without a moment's respite, body bristling in agitation. And so, with the acuity of the morbid logic she spun inside her cage, she destroyed the tissues of her own lungs more and more rapidly each passing day.

Her limbs, once round and smooth, grew thin as bamboo. A tap on her chest produced a hollow sound, like tapping on a doll made of thin papier-mâché. Eventually, not even her beloved giblets could get a reaction out of her.

To stimulate her appetite, he lined up all kinds of fish fresh from the sea along the veranda overlooking the garden, and told her about each one.

"Here's a monkfish, the clown of the sea, exhausted from dancing. And these armored fellows are kuruma shrimp, the fallen warriors of the deep. This horse mackerel is a leaf blown ashore in a windstorm."

"I'd rather listen to you read the Bible," she said.

Struck by an ominous premonition, he paused with the fish in his hand like Paul the Apostle and looked at his wife.

"I don't want to eat anything anymore. I just want you to read me the Bible, once a day."

And so, from that day on, he had no choice but to pull out the scruffy tome and start reading for her.

"Hear my prayer, O Lord, and let my cry come unto thee. Hide not thy face from me in the day when I am in trouble; incline thine ear unto me: in the day when I call answer me speedily. For my days are consumed like smoke, and my bones are burned as an hearth. My heart is smitten, and withered like grass; so that I forget to eat my bread."

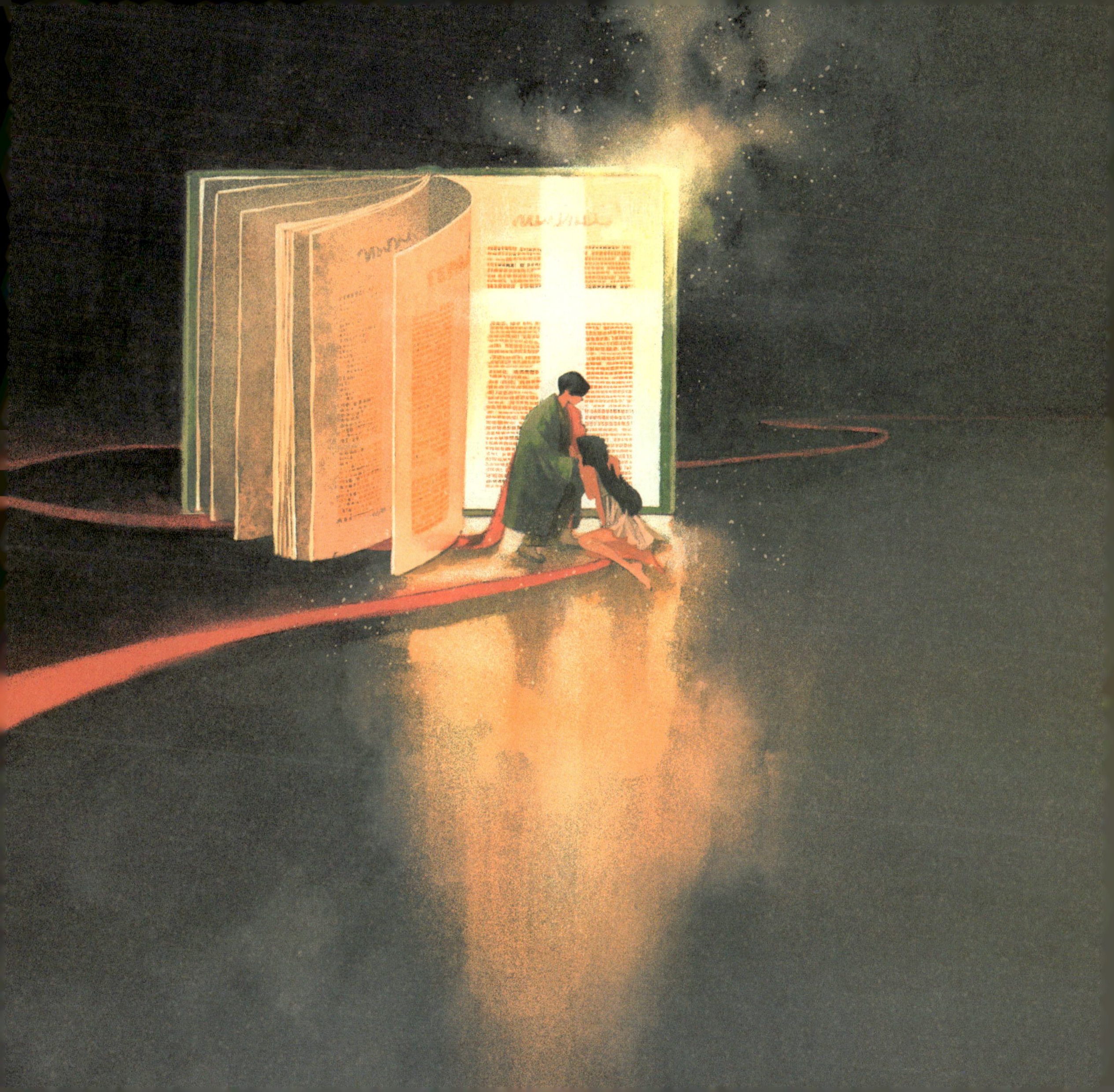

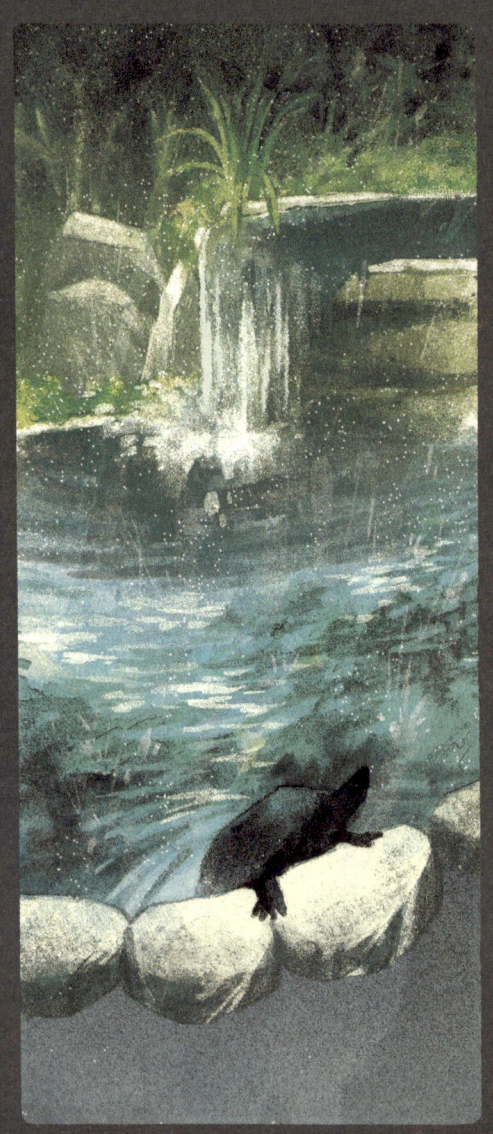

Yet that was not the last ominous sign. One morning, after a stormy night, he found that the sluggish turtle had disappeared from the garden pond.

As his wife's condition deteriorated, it became even more difficult for him to leave her side. She began to bring up phlegm every minute or so, and since she couldn't get rid of the stuff herself, it fell on him to wipe it from her mouth. She complained of excruciating stomach pains. Violent fits of coughing seized her about five times a day, regardless of the hour; each time, she clawed at her chest, moaning in agony. He felt he must keep calm in direct contrast to her suffering. But the more composed he became, the more she upbraided him, even as she coughed and writhed.

"How could you? How could you think of anything else while I'm going through such torture?"

"Quiet now, you mustn't shout like that."

"But look at you, so cool and collected—it's maddening."

"One of us needs to stay calm."

"You bastard!"

Snatching the scrap of tissue from his hand, she dragged it across her mouth to wipe away the phlegm, then flung it at him.

With one hand he toweled away the sweat that drenched her from head to toe, while with the other he had to continually wipe the sputum she coughed up. His back grew numb from bending over her. In her agony, she thrashed about and pummeled his chest with both hands, glowering up at the ceiling all the while. When the towel he was using to wipe away her sweat got caught in her nightgown, she kicked off the blanket and convulsed in wild waves, attempting to rise.

"Stop, stay still."

"It hurts, I can't breathe."

"Calm down."

"I'm in pain."

"You're only making it worse."

"Shut up!"

As she battered him like a shield, he gently stroked the sandpapery skin of her chest.

Even at the height of this agony, however, it occurred to him that her present suffering was in fact several degrees gentler than the crushing jealousy she had caused him before she fell ill. He realized that her declining body, with its rotting lungs, was bringing him more happiness than her healthy body had ever done.

This is new. There's nothing left for me but to cling to this novel way of looking at it.

Every time he called this new interpretation to mind, he burst into loud guffaws, gazing out at the sea.

And when he did, his wife would haul out the suspicious theories of the caged once again and eye him with disgust.

"Fine. I'm perfectly aware of why you're laughing, you know."

"The thing is, when I think how you'd want to get all dressed up in Western clothes and go gallivanting about after you got better, I can't tell you how grateful I am to have you lying here quietly like this. First off, there's an air of grace about you when you're so pale and still. Now just stay in bed and rest."

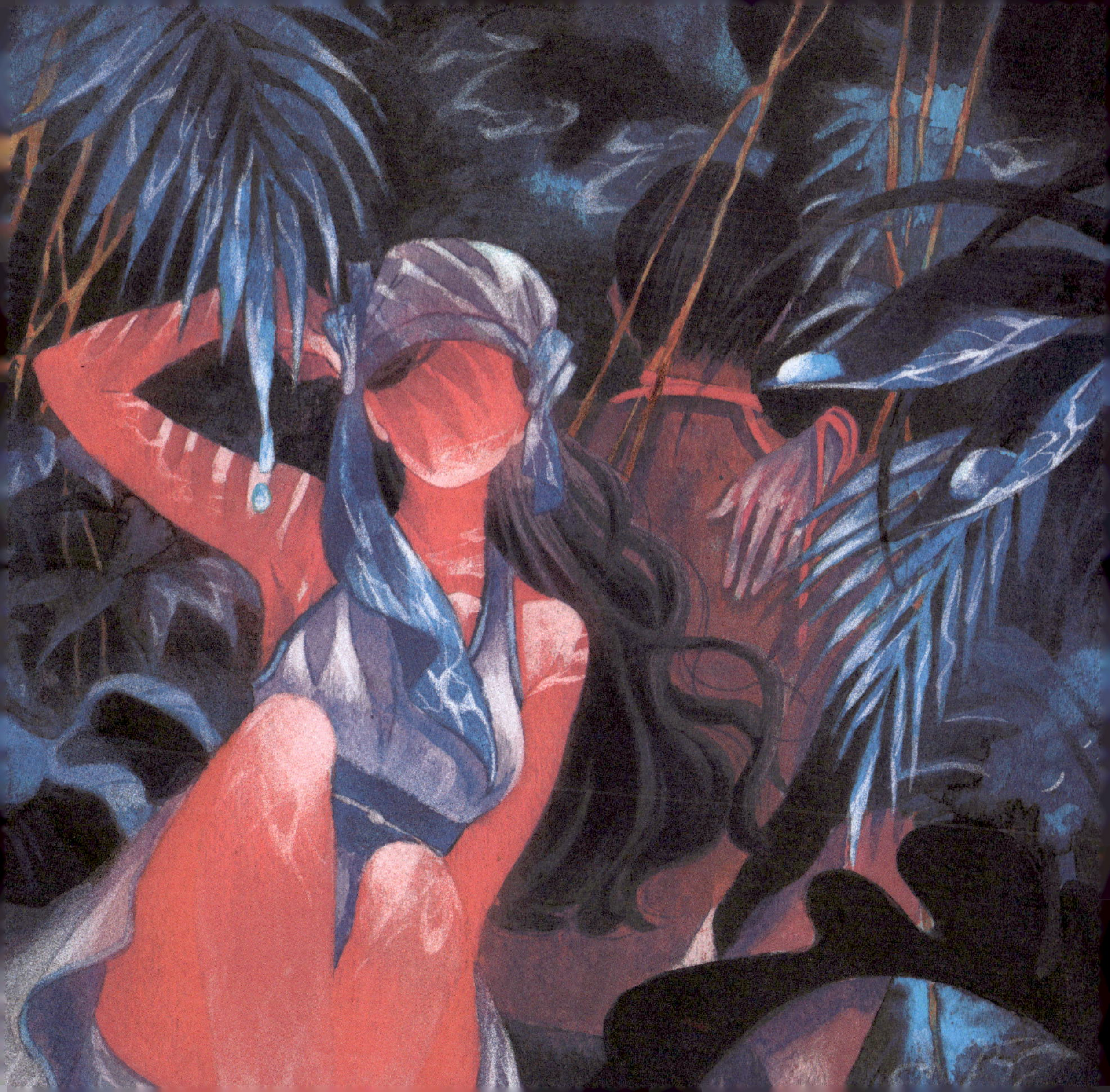

"Isn't that just like you."

"*Only* someone like me would be grateful to nurse an invalid."

"Do you have to bring that up every other word?"

"It's my point of pride."

"If this is how you're going to nurse me, I want none of it."

"But look what happens when I go into the other room, even just for three minutes—you act as though I'd abandoned you for three whole days. Well? Say something."

"All I'm asking is for you to look after me without griping. When you're making a face or moaning about how bothersome it is, I can't say I really feel grateful at all."

"But nursing someone is inherently bothersome, that's just the way it is."

"You think I don't know that? I just wish you'd keep quiet about it."

"Right then, well, I suppose I should drag all our friends and family into it, pile up a million yen, and hire ten doctors and a hundred nurses."

"I don't want anything of the kind. I want you, and only you, to take care of me."

"In other words, you're telling me to play the part of ten doctors, a hundred nurses, and a wealthy benefactor all by myself, is that it?"

"That's not what I meant at all. If only you could just stay by my side, I could rest easy."

"Well, there you are. I might complain or frown now and again, but you'll just have to put up with it."

"When I die, I'll curse you a thousand times before I go."

"I think I can handle that."

His wife said nothing more. But in that silence, he could sense her feverishly sharpening her thoughts to a keen edge, preparing for her next attack.

In the meantime, he also had to worry about his own work and life, which in turn exacerbated her illness. But he was gradually growing exhausted from nursing his wife, and from lack of sleep. He knew full well that the more tired he was, the less able he was to work. And of course, the less he worked, the more difficult it became to make ends meet. There was nothing he could do about the fact that the mounting costs of caring for his ailing wife increased in direct proportion to the strain on his living. Moreover, it was inevitable that whatever else happened, the passing days would only drain him more and more.

So what am I supposed to do?

Just strike me down, too. At this point I'd die willingly, lacking for nothing. I'd show you how it's done.

His thoughts sometimes strayed down this path. Yet he also felt an urge to see with his own eyes how he would pull through this crisis, to get one clear glimpse of his own capability. Whenever he was awoken in the night, it became his habit to mutter, "Let more misery be piled on me, let more misery be piled on me," as he stroked his wife's aching belly. In such moments, the image of a vast sea of felt rose into his mind, a solitary ball, struck by the cue, rolling aimlessly across it.

That's my ball.
But who made such a
poor shot with it?

"Rub harder, dear. When
did you get so lazy? You weren't
always like that. You used to be more
kind and attentive when you rubbed my
stomach. But now—oh, it hurts, it hurts,"
she cried.

"I'm getting worn out, too. I reckon
I'll break down soon, myself. Then the
two of us will be able to laze here side
by side."

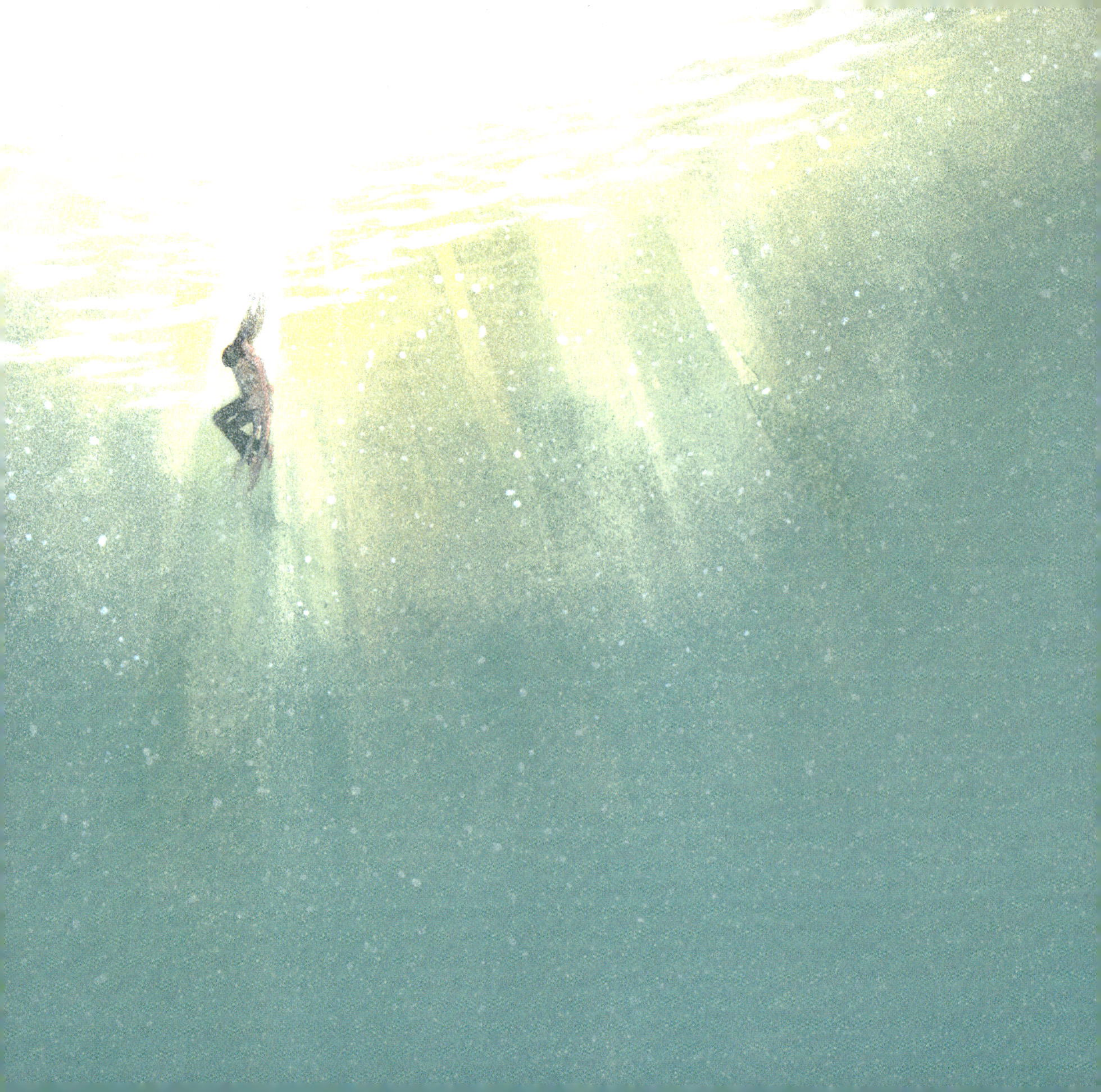

At this, she suddenly fell still, and, in a pitiful voice like an insect chirping under the floorboards, she murmured, "I've been terribly selfish toward you all this time. Now I'm ready to die at any moment. I'm satisfied. Please, dear, you go to sleep. I'll bear up."

When he heard this, he wept in spite of himself, and he no longer wished to rest the hand that stroked her stomach.

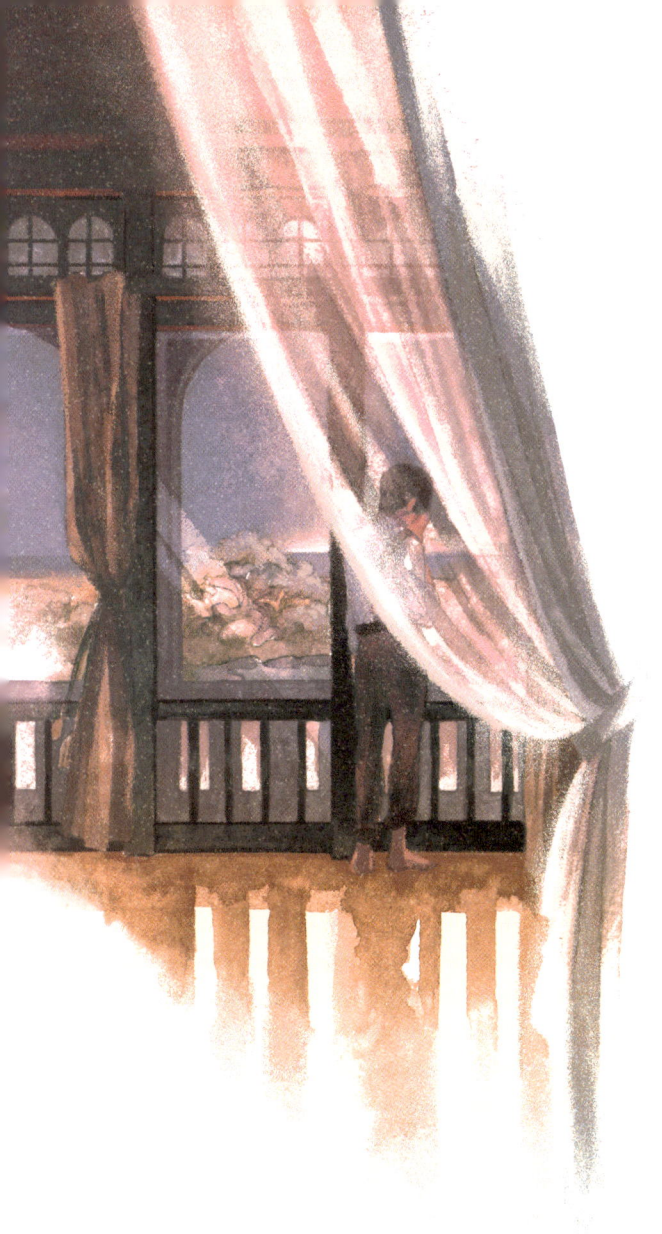

The grass in the garden withered under the winter winds that blew in from the sea. All day long, the glass panes on the sliding doors of the house trembled and rattled like the windows of a hackney carriage. He had long forgotten that the vast ocean lay just outside the house.

One day, he went to the doctor's to get more medicine for his wife.

"You know, I've been meaning to tell you for a while now," the doctor began. "But at this point, there's no hope for her."

"Ah." He could feel the color draining from his face.

"Her left lung is already gone, and the right one is well on its way."

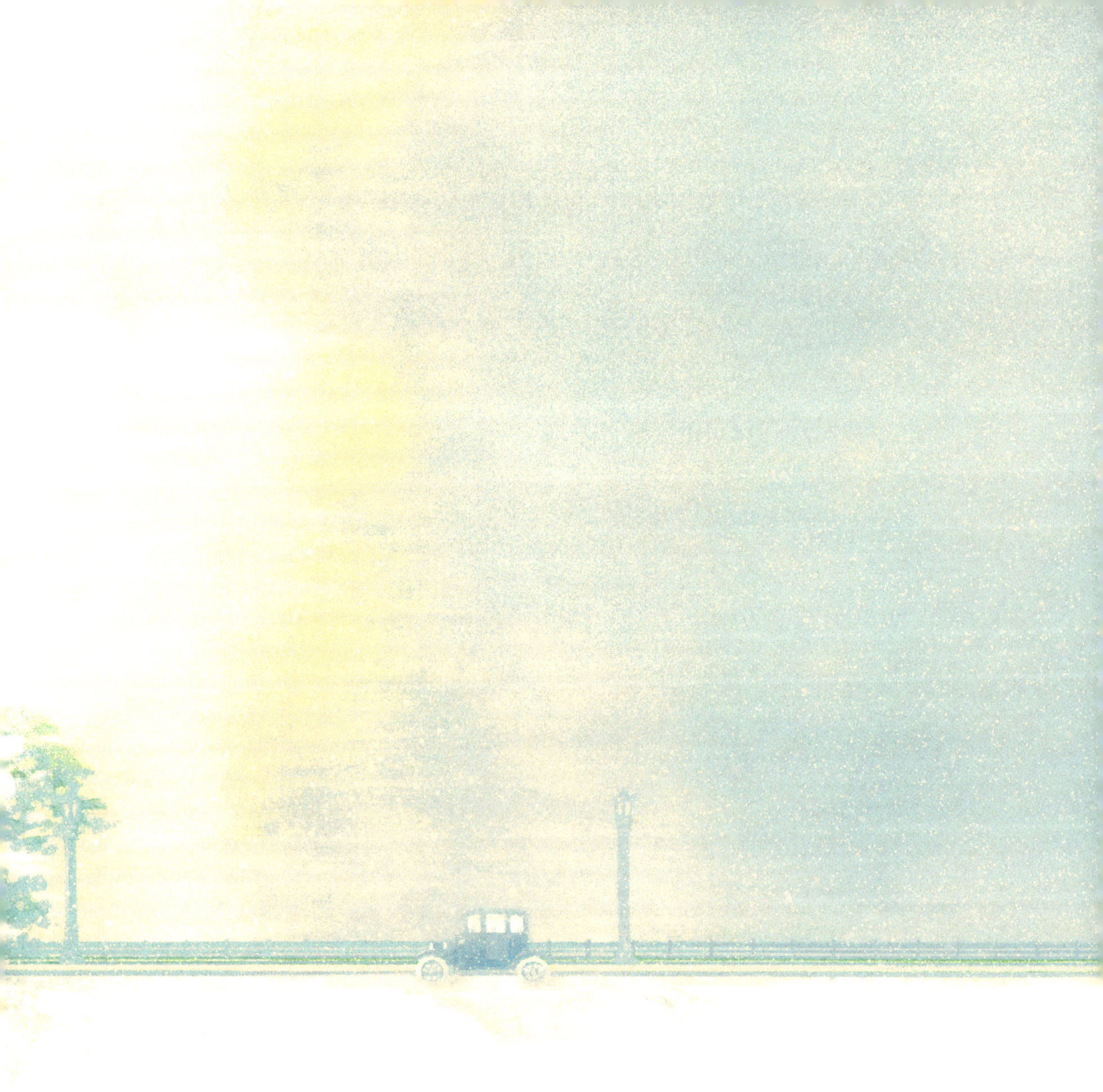

He went back home along the seashore in a car, jostled about like a piece of luggage. The clear, bright ocean unfurled before him, hanging languidly like a uniform curtain that hid death from his view. He thought he never wanted to see his wife again. If he didn't look at her, he felt certain he could carry on feeling her living presence forever.

When he got home, he headed straight for his room. There he mulled over how he could avoid seeing his wife's face. Stepping out into the garden, he lay down on the lawn. Fatigue weighed down his body, heavy and spent.

As tears trickled weakly down his face, he plucked out the shriveled blades of grass one by one.

"What is death?"

To become hidden from view, he thought. *Nothing more.* After a while, he quelled the turmoil in his heart and went into his wife's sickroom.

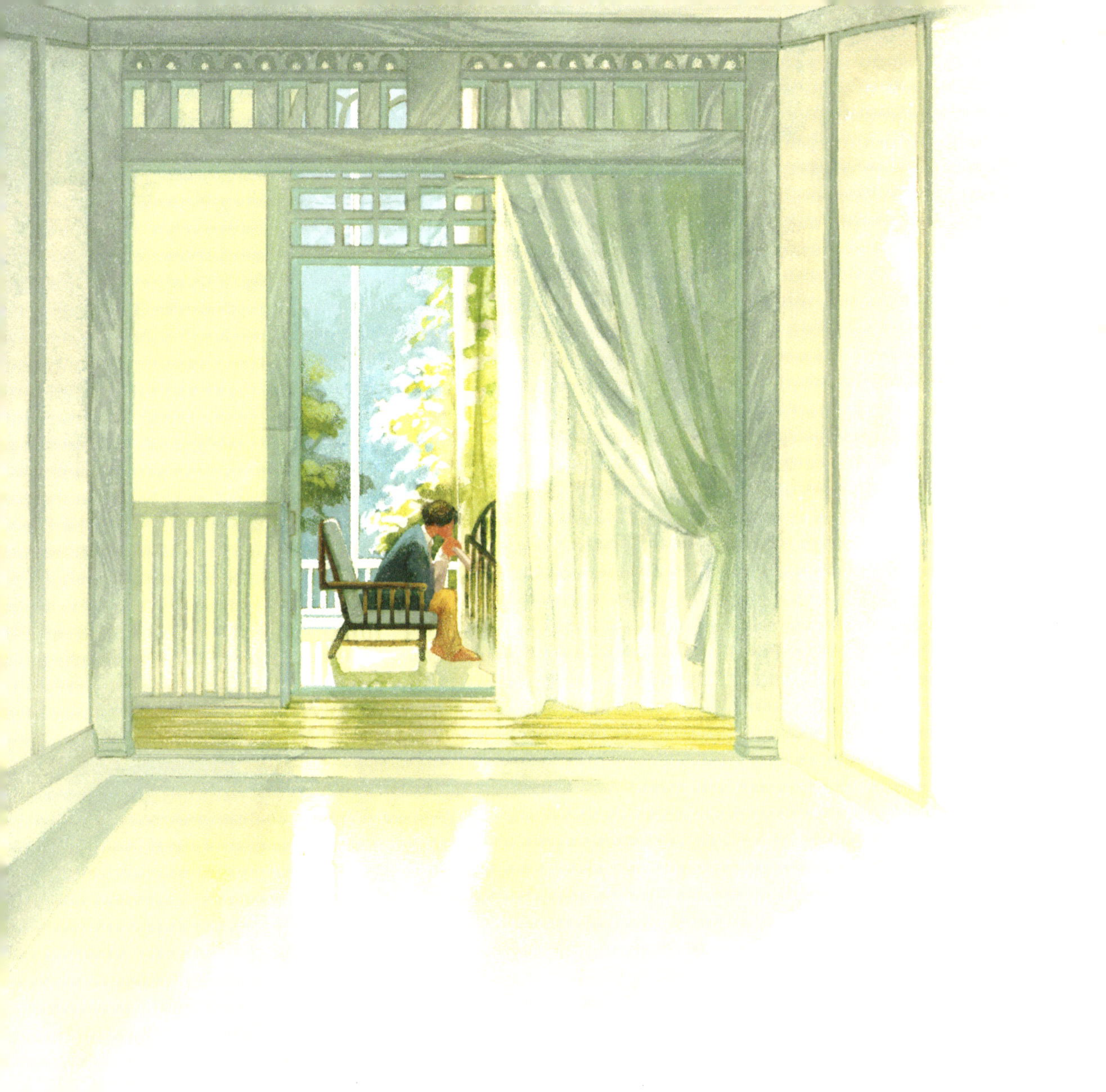

She stared at his face in silence.

"Shall I get you some winter flowers?"

"You've been crying, dear," she said.

"No."

"Yes, you have."

"What reason do I have to cry?"

"I know what happened. The doctor said something, didn't he?"

Without waiting for a reply, she silently turned her gaze to the ceiling. There was no sadness in her face. He sat down in the wicker chair beside her pillow and stared at her intently, as if to burn her face into his memory afresh.

Soon, the door between us will be closed.

But both of us have given the other everything we have to give. There's nothing left now.

From that day on, he did everything she asked, like a machine. He considered this his final parting gift to her.

One day, after a violent fit of pain, his wife said to him, "Dear, could you get me some morphine next time?"

"What will you do with it?"

"I'll drink it. I've heard if you drink morphine, you go to sleep and never wake up again."

"Die, you mean?"

"Yes. I'm not afraid of dying, not at all. I can't imagine how wonderful it will be to die."

"When did you become so wise? Once a person reaches that point, they truly are ready to die."

"But, you know, I feel badly for you. I've caused you nothing but pain. I'm sorry."

He gave a noncommittal little grunt.

"I know your heart like the back of my hand. But all my selfish demands, that wasn't me. It was my sickness making me speak."

"That's right. It was the sickness."

"I've already written up a will and everything. I won't show it to you now, though. It's under my bed, you can look at it after I'm gone."

He said nothing. *The truth is sad enough as it is,* he thought. *I wish you wouldn't say things that make it even worse.*

The dahlia bulbs, dug up and abandoned beside the stones of the flower bed, were rotting in the frost. In place of the turtle, a stray cat had wandered in from who knows where, and it got up and began prowling around his empty study. His wife was in too much pain to speak most of the time. She merely gazed at the distant, glinting cape where it thrust out over the surface of the ocean toward the horizon.

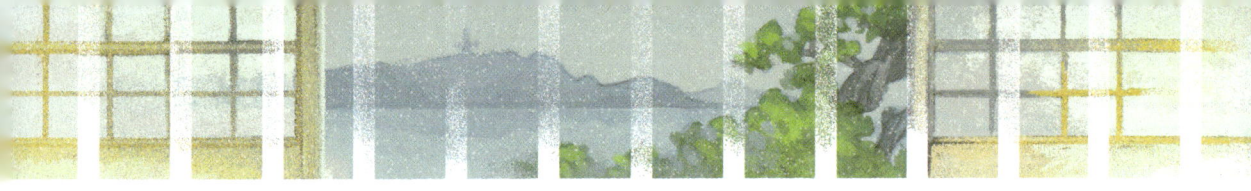

Sometimes he sat beside her and read aloud from the Bible, as she had asked.

"O Lord, rebuke me not in thine anger, neither chasten me in thy hot displeasure. Have mercy upon me, O Lord; for I am weak: O Lord, heal me; for my bones are vexed. My soul is also sore vexed: but thou, O Lord, how long? For in death there is no remembrance of thee."

He heard his wife weeping softly. Putting down the Bible, he looked at her. "What were you thinking just now?"

"Where will my bones end up? I just wish I knew."

In this moment, in her heart of hearts, it's her bones that concern her.

He couldn't bring himself to answer.

It's over.

His heart sank along with his drooping head.

At this, the tears gushed even more fiercely from her eyes.

"What is it?"

"My bones have nowhere to go. What should I do?"

Instead of responding, he hurriedly began to read another passage from the Bible.

"Save me, O God; for the waters are come in unto my soul. I sink in deep mire, where there is no standing: I am come into deep waters, where the floods overflow me. I am weary of my crying: my throat is dried: mine eyes fail while I wait for my God."

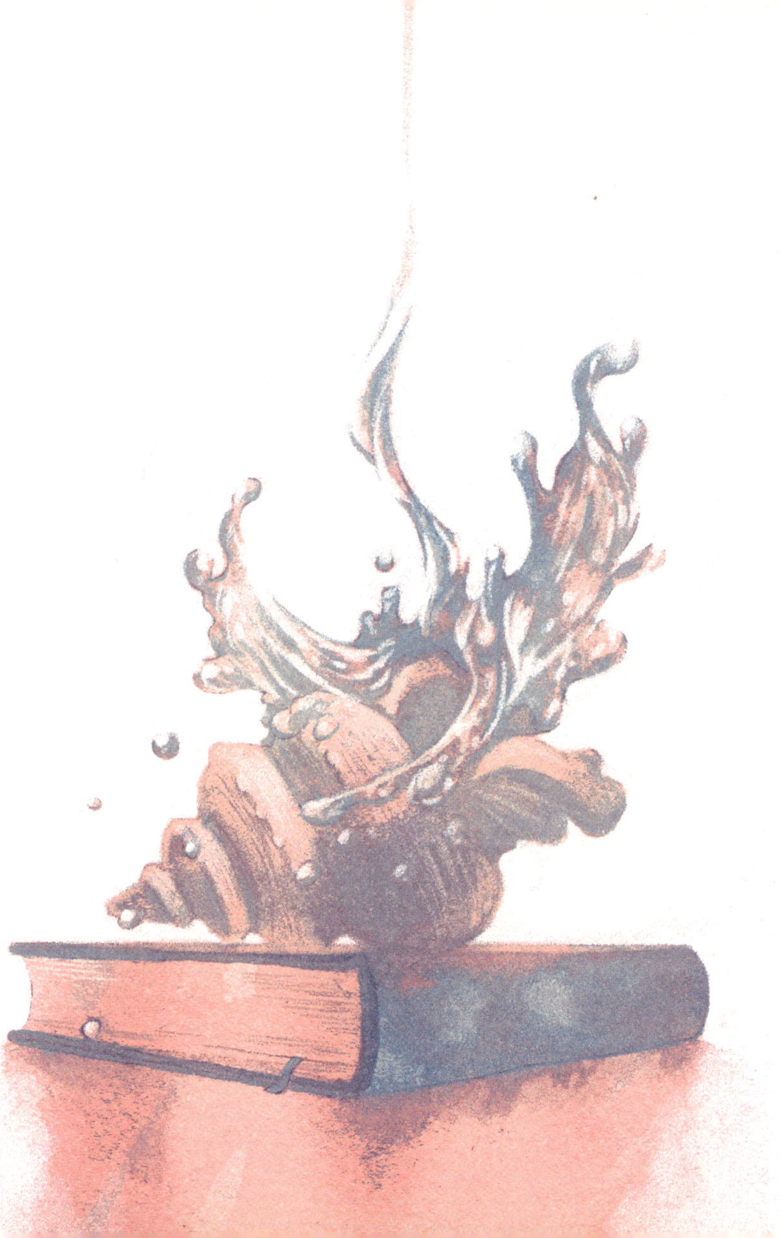

He and his wife spent the days lying silently side by side like a pair of withered stems. By now, however, they had both made the last of their preparations for death. Come what may, they had nothing more to fear. There amid the hush of his dark house, the earthen jug of water brought from the mountains brimmed as clear and untainted as a serene heart.

Each morning, while his wife slept, he walked barefoot along the new land that reared its head above the surface of the ocean. His feet got tangled in the seaweed washed ashore by last night's high tide. Some days, the children who lived by the sea wandered out as though blown by the wind, slipping on the carpet of vivid green laver as they clambered up the rocks.

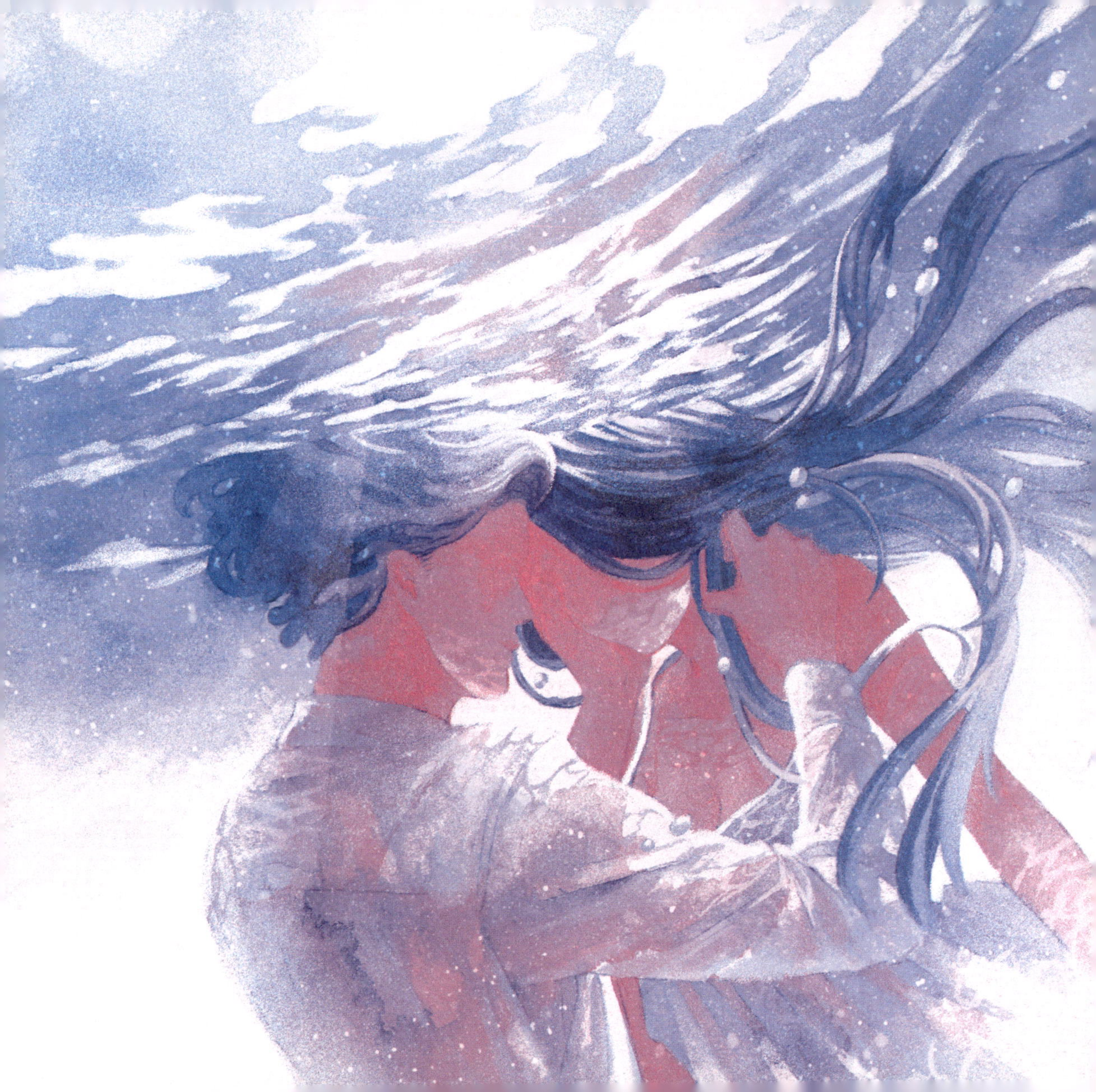

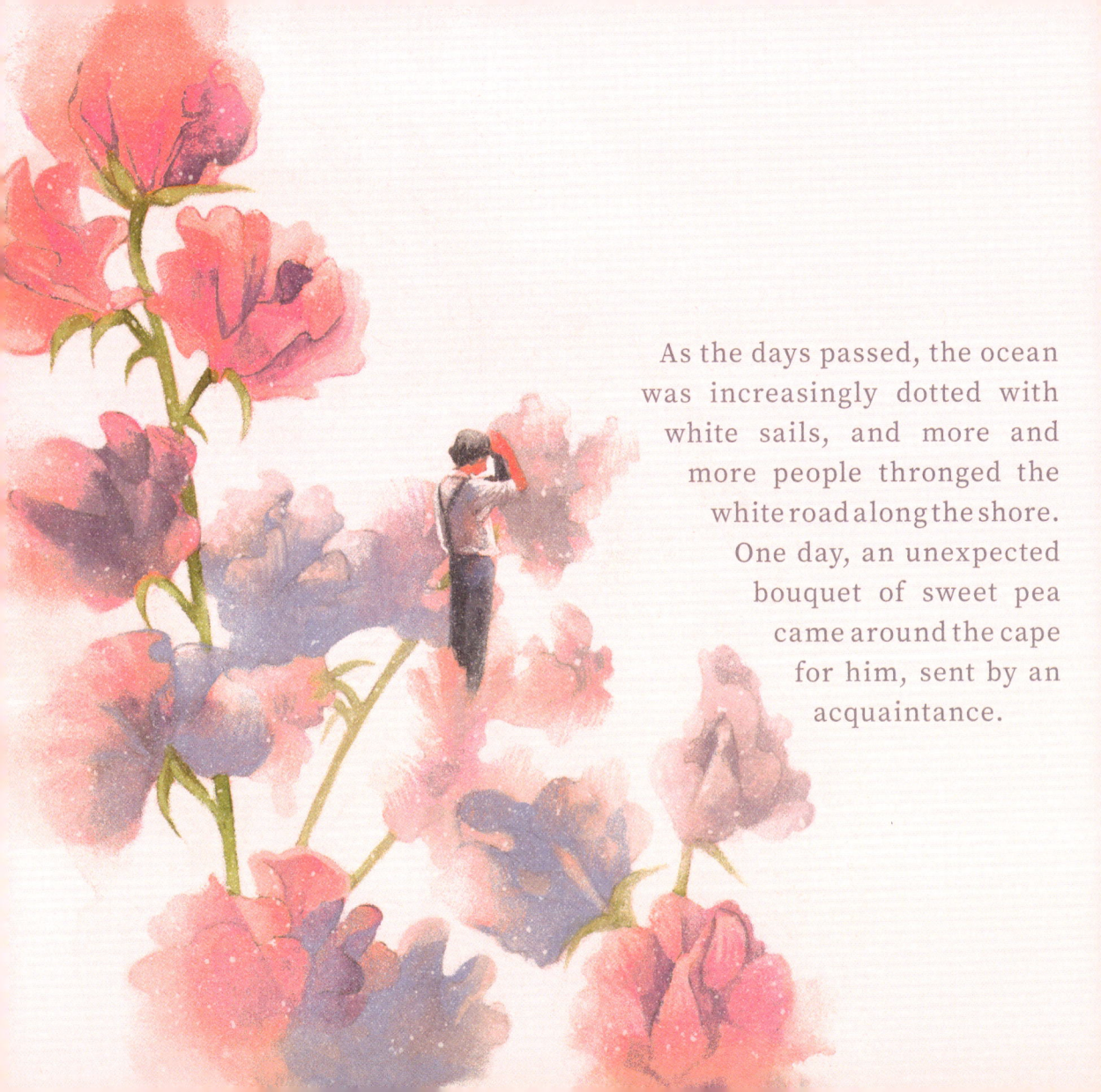

As the days passed, the ocean was increasingly dotted with white sails, and more and more people thronged the white road along the shore. One day, an unexpected bouquet of sweet pea came around the cape for him, sent by an acquaintance.

The house, long desolate and battered by icy winds, was at last visited by this beautiful, fragrant messenger of early spring.

Holding the flowers like an offering in his pollen-covered hands, he went into his wife's room.

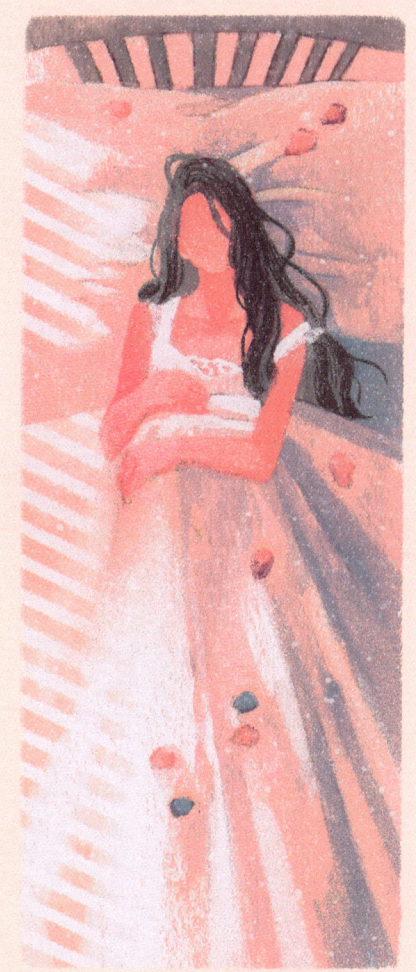

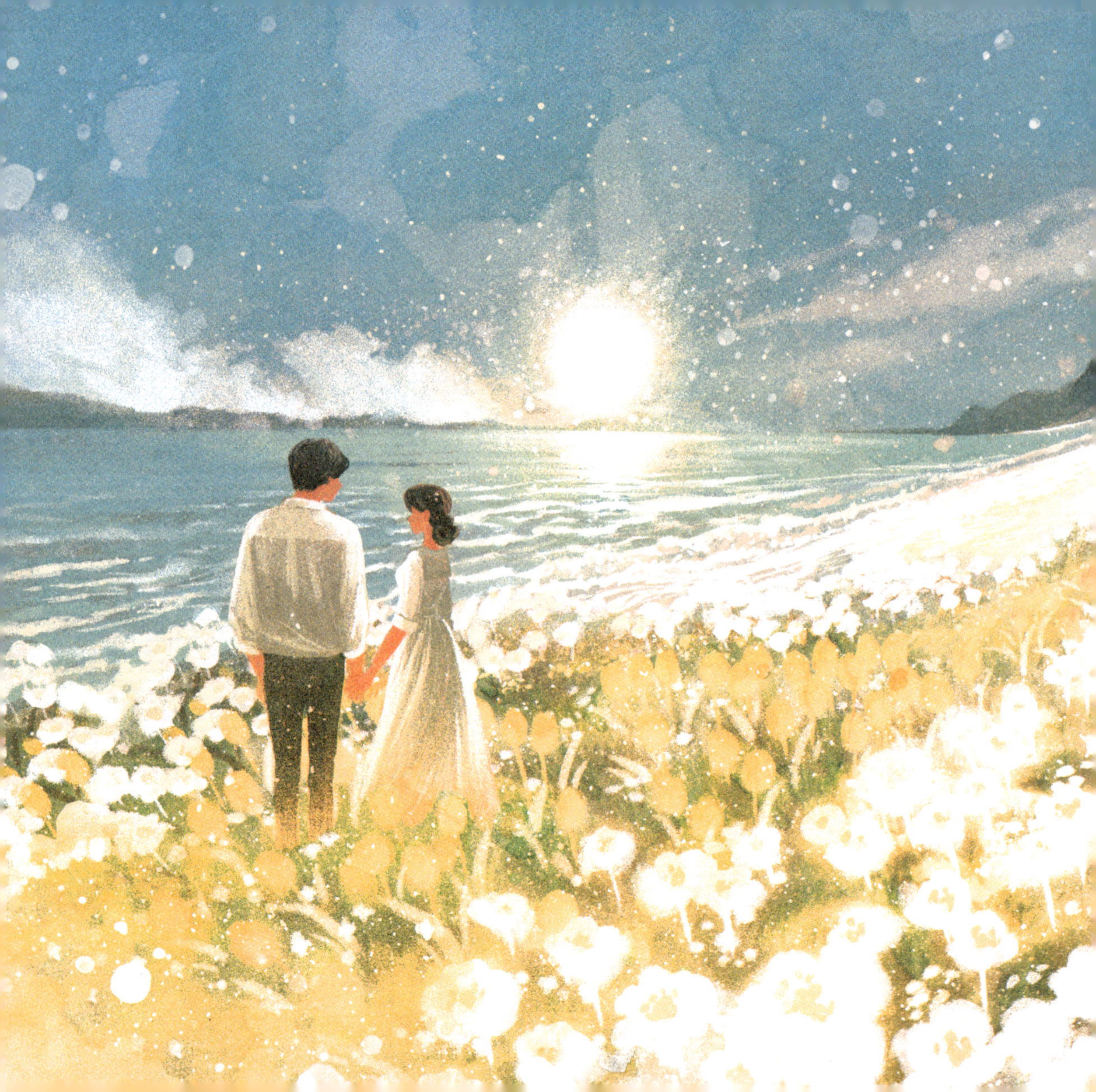

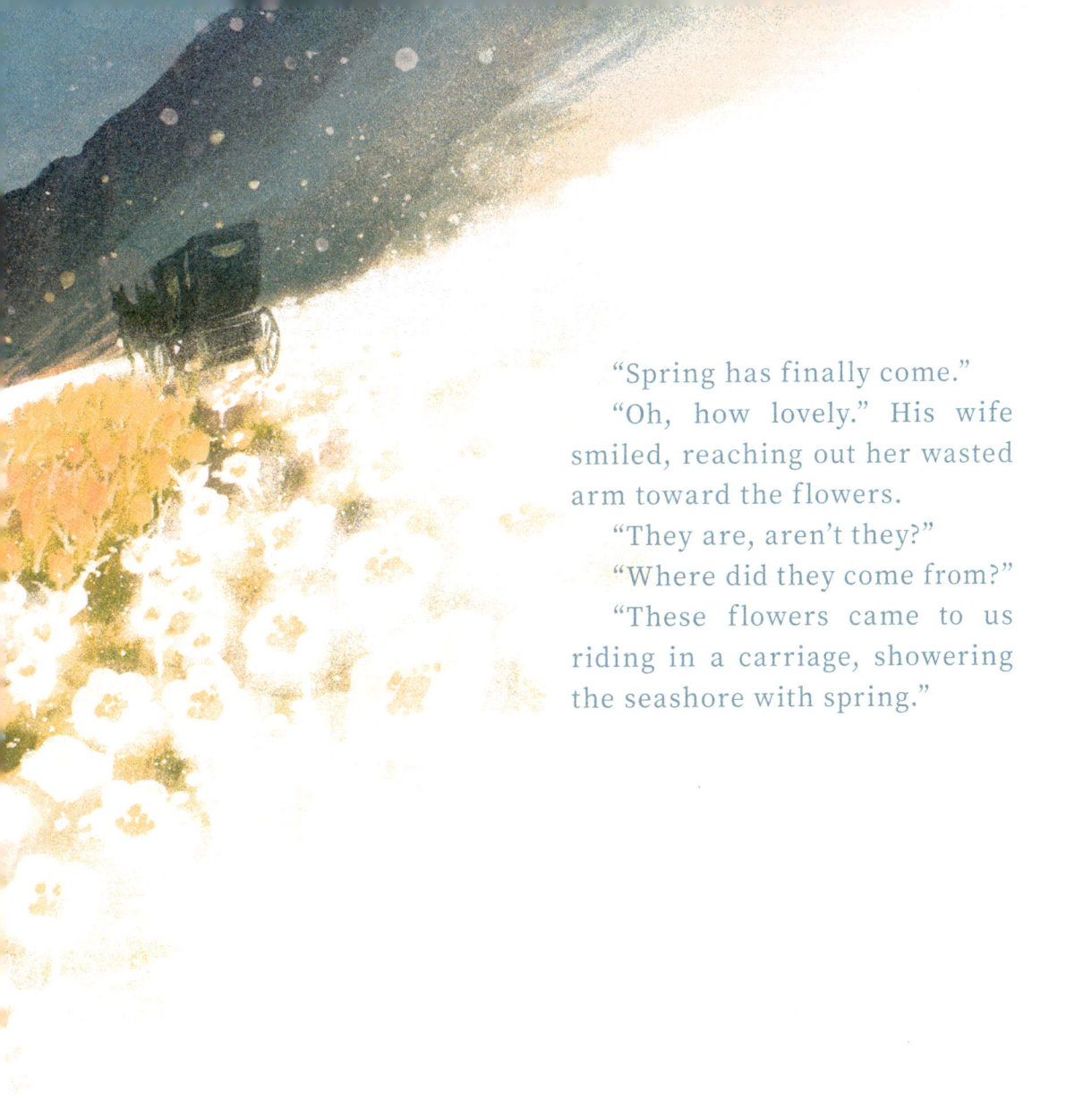

"Spring has finally come."

"Oh, how lovely." His wife smiled, reaching out her wasted arm toward the flowers.

"They are, aren't they?"

"Where did they come from?"

"These flowers came to us riding in a carriage, showering the seashore with spring."

His wife took the bouquet from him and held it tight to her chest with both hands. Then, burying her pallid face in the bright spray of flowers, she closed her eyes in rapture.

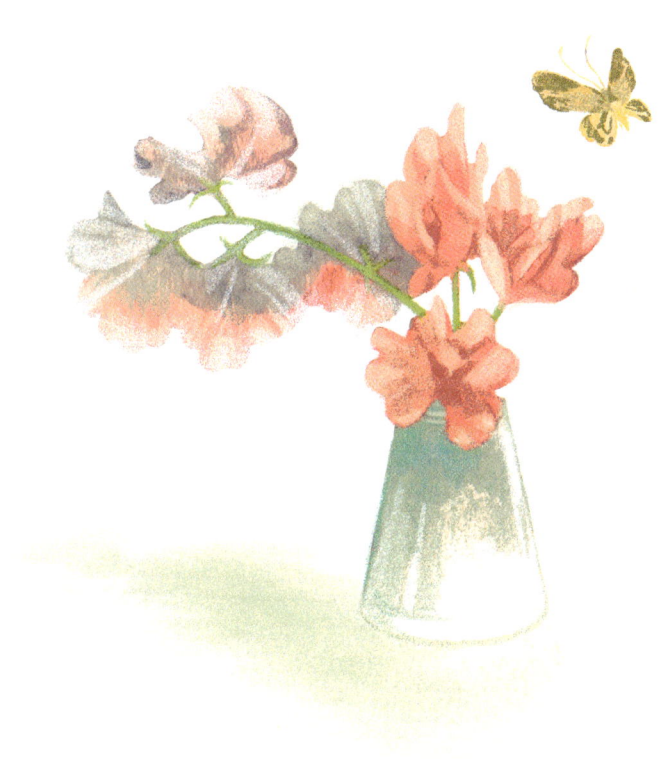

This book may include language that could be seen as offensive or discriminatory from today's standpoint, but in the interest of preserving the historical import of the work, we have included it in its original form.

Maiden's Bookshelf

Spring Comes Riding in a Carriage

A VERTICAL Book

Translation: Yui Kajita
Editor: Daniel Joseph
Production: Risa Cho
Proofreading: Kevin Luo

HARU HA BASHA NI NOTTE written by Riichi Yokomitsu, illustrated by Atsuki Ito
Copyright © 2021 Atsuki Ito

All rights reserved.
Original Japanese edition published by Rittorsha.

This English edition published by arrangement with Rittor Music, Inc., Tokyo
in care of Tuttle-Mori Agency, Inc., Tokyo.

English language version produced by Kodansha USA Publishing, LLC, 2023

This is a work of fiction.

ISBN: 978-1-64729-182-2

Printed in the United States of America

First Edition

Kodansha USA Publishing, LLC
451 Park Avenue South
7th Floor
New York, NY 10016
www.kodansha.us

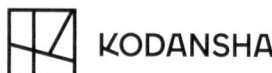